Helen Orme taught for many years before giving up teaching to write full-time. At the last count she had written over 70 books.

She writes both fiction and non-fiction, but at present is concentrating on fiction for older readers.

Helen also runs writing workshops for children and courses for teachers in both primary and secondary schools.

How many have you read?

Horsing
Around

Helen Orme

Rans**m**

Horsing Around

by Helen Orme
Illustrated by Cathy Brett
Cover by Anna Torborg

Published by Ransom Publishing Ltd.
51 Southgate Street, Winchester, Hants. SO23 9EH
www.ransom.co.uk

ISBN   978 184167 685 2
First published in 2007
Copyright © 2007 Ransom Publishing Ltd.

Illustrations copyright © 2007 Cathy Brett and Anna Torborg

Meet the Sisters ...

Siti and her friends are really close. So close she calls them her Sisters. They've been mates for ever, and most of the time they are closer than her real family.

Siti is the leader – the one who always knows what to do – but Kelly, Lu, Donna and Rachel have their own lives to lead as well.

Still, there's no one you can talk to, no one you can rely on, like your best mates. Right?

1

The worst thing he could have said

At the end of every summer term there was a whole week when they all got to choose what they wanted to do.

"What do you want to do?" Siti asked her friends.

Siti and the others had been friends for ever! They were so close that they called themselves 'The Sisters'.

"I'm going to ask if I can go to the stables," said Donna.

"What a surprise!" said Rachel.

Donna was really very good at riding and had won lots of cups and things. She worked at the stables whenever she could.

"I'm going to do community work," said Rachel. "Why don't you do that too, Siti?"

"I might," said Siti. "I'm still thinking."

"We're going on the Outdoor Activities course," said Lu.

"It will be really good. We're going camping for two nights," added Kelly.

Donna had spoken to Mrs Samways, the lady who ran the stables.

"Of course," she said. "I'd love to have you for a week. Why don't you ask your teachers if two or three of your friends can come too?"

Donna tried to get one of the others to go with her, but they all wanted to do their own things.

She told Mr Lester, their form tutor, what Mrs Samways had said.

"Good," he said. "I need somewhere for Kathryn, Sarah and Laura. I'll ring Mrs Samways today."

Donna looked at him with horror. That was just about the worst thing he could have said.

2

Friends?

"I hate those three," said Donna. She was telling the others all about it. "That Kathryn is so stuck up and Laura is always nasty to me. Can't at least one of you lot come instead? Please."

Siti felt sorry for Donna, so she went to Mr Lester and asked to change.

"I'm sorry," he said. "But I can't change it now – everything is fixed. I know that Kathryn doesn't get on well with Donna, but I don't think Donna has anything to worry about. After all, she is a really good rider now."

It was the start of activities week. Lu and Kelly were having a day to get ready for camping, Siti and Rachel were visiting the local hospital and Donna had gone to the stables.

She was really unhappy, but she soon cheered up when she started work. She just loved the horses so much.

She was there early. Mrs Samways was pleased to see her.

"Can you start with mucking out, please?" she said. "Then you can have some time to practice your jumping for the next show."

Donna had been working hard. She was hot and dirty – and smelly! Then Kathryn and her friends arrived. Mrs Samways brought them down to her.

"Your friends are here, Donna," she said.

"If only!" thought Donna, but she tried to make an effort and smiled at them. "Hello."

Kathryn looked at her. "Oh hello," she said, without smiling.

Behind Mrs Samways' back, Sarah was holding her nose.

"We're going to have a cup of tea now," said Mrs Samways. "Have you finished?"

"Just about," said Donna. "I'll come in a minute."

3

Saddle up

When Donna got to the office, Kathryn was talking – loudly, as she always did.

"Oh yes, I've done lots of riding. My cousin has two ponies and I always ride when I go to see her."

"What about you two?" asked Mrs Samways. "Have you done much?"

"A bit," said Sarah.

"Some," said Laura.

"Good – we'll saddle up and go for a quick trot."

"What's *she* going to do?" asked Laura, looking at Donna.

"Oh, Donna needs to practice for the next show. After I've seen you ride, you can go and watch her for a while."

"No thanks!" Laura whispered to Sarah. "I think we can do better than that, don't you?"

Donna went off to saddle up her favourite horse. He was called Bluey and he was really gentle. He loved Donna and she always made a special fuss of him. As soon as she was outside on Bluey, she forgot about Kathryn and the other two.

After a warm-up she started to work on the jumps. They weren't very high, but she needed to make sure that Bluey knew exactly where to land.

Mrs Samways had chosen well-behaved horses for the other three. She wanted to see how good they were. Kathryn was quite good, but the other two were awful!

"Well," she thought to herself. "At least I'll have plenty of help with the mucking out, and Donna can help them out a bit so they get some riding practice while they're here."

"Let's go and watch Donna now," she suggested.

At the end of the day, they all went back on the bus together. Donna sat on her own. The others sat in front of her.

4

Making things worse

They weren't very happy. Mrs Samways had explained that they would have to do mucking out, help feed the horses and clean the equipment.

"I can't let you ride alone," she had said. "But I'll give you some time when I'm not too busy."

Sarah glared at Donna. "It's all her fault," she said loudly. "Mr Lester would never have thought about it if it hadn't been for her."

"Mucking out – ugh!" agreed Laura. "It will ruin my jeans, and they're designer gear, you know."

"It's all right for her," said Kathryn. "She's used to living in a mess – I mean, have you seen where she lives!"

"You ride much better than she does," said Sarah. "I don't know why Mrs S thinks she's so great. You need to show them both just what you can do."

"I might just do that," said Kathryn.

By the time they got off the bus, Donna was nearly in tears.

She rang Siti that night.

Siti tried to cheer her up, but there was nothing she could do.

"Tell Mrs Samways," she said. But Donna didn't want to do that.

By the middle of the week, Donna was really fed up. Kathryn and her friends kept on and on at her. They said she smelt of horse, they said her clothes were manky, they said she was no good.

One of the problems was that Mrs Samways was getting fed up with them. Even though Donna didn't say anything, Mrs Samways could see what was going on.

She talked to them.

"If this doesn't stop, I'm going to send you back to school," she said.

The trouble was, it didn't help. It just made things worse!

5

"Watch me!"

Kathryn was fed up with the stables, she was fed up with muck and she wanted to ride. She really did like horses and she wanted to ride her favourite – a beautiful mare called Sharry. Sharry was very pretty but she was very nervous. Mrs Samways was training her herself and wouldn't let anyone else ride her.

Kathryn talked to Sarah and Laura.

"If she's going to send us back to school, then it doesn't matter what we do," she said.

"When Mrs S is teaching this afternoon, I'm going to get Sharry out and ride her."

"She'll see you," said Laura.

"No she won't," said Kathryn. "She's taking this group along the track through the woods."

They waited until Mrs Samways was out of sight. Donna was riding Bluey in the paddock and Jim, who was in charge when Mrs Samways wasn't around, was having a cup of tea in the office.

Kathryn, Sarah and Laura went into Sharry's stall and got her ready to ride. Kathryn led her out and got on.

"Watch me!" she called, as she set off along the driveway.

Donna heard them and looked over to see what was happening. She knew that Kathryn shouldn't be riding Sharry.

She opened the paddock gate and rode towards her.

Just at that moment, something terrible happened. The feed lorry turned into the gate.

The driver saw Kathryn and hooted.

Sharry spooked. She started to gallop – towards the open gate!

6

A hero

Donna was already riding towards Kathryn. She heard the hooting, and then she heard Kathryn scream. She knew she would never catch up with Sharry, but, thinking fast, she headed straight towards the open gate. Bluey raced as fast as he could.

The lorry had stopped. Sarah and Laura were screaming too and Jim had rushed out of the office.

It was all over in a few moments. Sharry was fast, but she didn't really know what she was doing. Donna and Bluey worked well together – they always did – and they reached the gate before Sharry. Donna headed Sharry away from the gate and shouted to Kathryn to tell her what to do.

She and Bluey galloped with Sharry and slowly she calmed down. Soon, Donna reached out and grabbed her bridle. They all stopped.

Kathryn got off. She was shaking so much she nearly fell. Luckily Jim arrived just in time to catch her.

Donna never found out what Mrs Samways said to the three.

Kathryn was sent home straight away. Sarah and Laura had to stay for the rest of the week and were made to work really hard.

Mrs Samways told Donna she was a hero.

"I hope that Kathryn will be grateful to you for saving her," she said. "Maybe she'll be nice to you after all this."

"Not likely," thought Donna. "I know her better than that! But at least the week's nearly over, and the Sisters will be together again. Being with the Sisters is even better than being with the horses!"